You Can Do It!

Written and Illustrated by
Gee Johnson

4

6

Up there? I can't get up there.

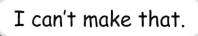

11

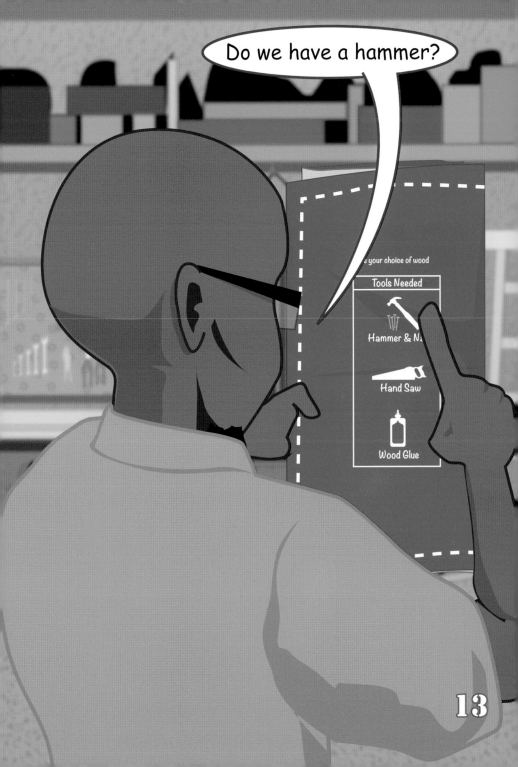

19

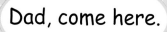

24

WORD ATTACK STRATEGIES
Tips for tricky words

Stop	**Stop** if something doesn't look right, sound right, or make sense.
	Look at the **picture**.
b_____	Say the **first letter** sound.
bl_____	**Blend:** Say the first two letters.
⟵	**Reread:** Go back and try again.

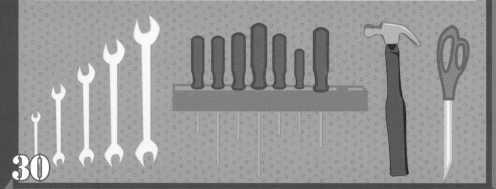

POWER WORDS

a	going	no	to
and	good	now	two
are	got	of	up
can	have	one	we
can't	here	out	we'll
come	I	see	will
dad	is	that	yes
did	it	the	you
do	let's	there	you'll
get	make	three	your

Word Match

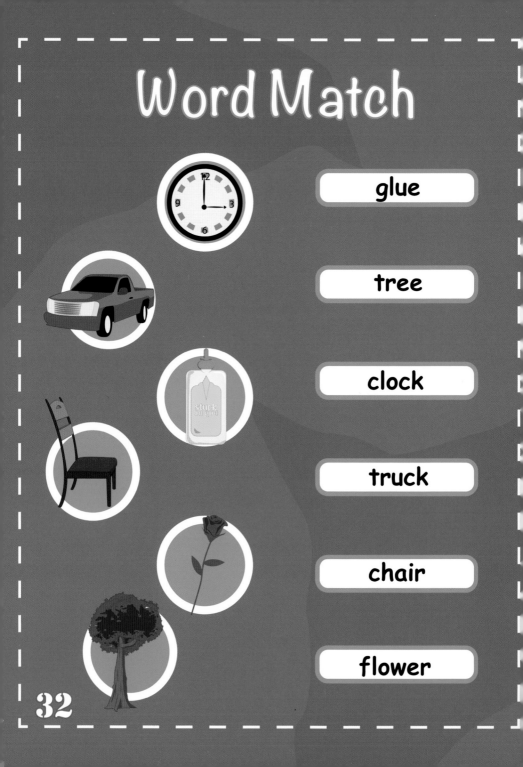

glue

tree

clock

truck

chair

flower